by William Joyce

A LAURA GERINGER BOOK
An Imprint of HarperCollins Publishers

Huge Robo-Thanks to:

The Nelvana Wonderkins,

Ian MacLeod, Jordan Thistlewood & Pam Lehn

and

Scott Dyer, Susie Grondin, Robert Padovan, Bill Giggie,

Ron Pitts, Mark Stanger

and El Director, Mike Fallows,

and, of course, the

Grand High Polie Pooh-bah,

Toper Taylor, Esq.

THE ROLIE POLIE OLIE ANIMATED TELEVISION SERIES
IS PRODUCED BY NELVANA LIMITED AND METAL HURLANT PRODUCTIONS SARL.

Library of Congress Cataloging-in-Publication Data
Joyce, William.   Rolie Polie Olie / by William Joyce.   p.   cm.   "A Laura Geringer book."
Summary: Rolie Polie Olie, a round robot living on a planet where everything is round,
enjoys a busy day with his family and then is too wired to go to bed at night.
ISBN 0-06-027163-9. — ISBN 0-06-027164-7 (lib. bdg.)
[1. Robots—Fiction.   2. Circle—Fiction.   3. Stories in rhyme.]   I. Title.
PZ8.3.J835Ro 1999   99-21176
[E]—dc21   CIP

Typography by Alicia Mikles
Production by Ruiko Tokunaga
1 2 3 4 5 6 7 8 9 10
❖
First Edition

To my
Rolie Polie Pal,
Jackson Edward
Joyce

Way up high
in the Rolie Polie Sky
is a little round planet
of a really swell guy.

He's Rolie Polie Olie—

He likes to laugh and play.

And in his land

of curves and curls,

this is how he spends his day. . . .

Rolie Polie Olie
rolled out of bed.

Brushed his teeth.

Recharged his head.

Downstairs he found his mom and pop,
his sister, Zowie; his doggy, Spot.

He filled his bowl with Rolie O's,
turned on the Rolie Radio. . . .

The Rolie Polie Rumba Dance

was always done in underpants!

Then Momma said,
"Chores must be done."
And Olie moaned,
"Oh, that's no fun!"
But Zowie helped,
and so did Pop.
They all jumped on
the hip-hop mop
and mopped the house
from tip to top!

They picked up toys
and folded clothes.
They washed up these
and watered those. . . .

"I just had
a **mess** of fun,"
said Olie when
the job was done.

They laughed, they raced, they hopped, they spun—

One for all and all for one!

The sun is high, the sky is blue.

It's afternoon—there's lots to do.

Howdy, Yard!

Howdy, Day!

Howdy, World!

Come on, let's play!

Swash and buckle, skip and glide.

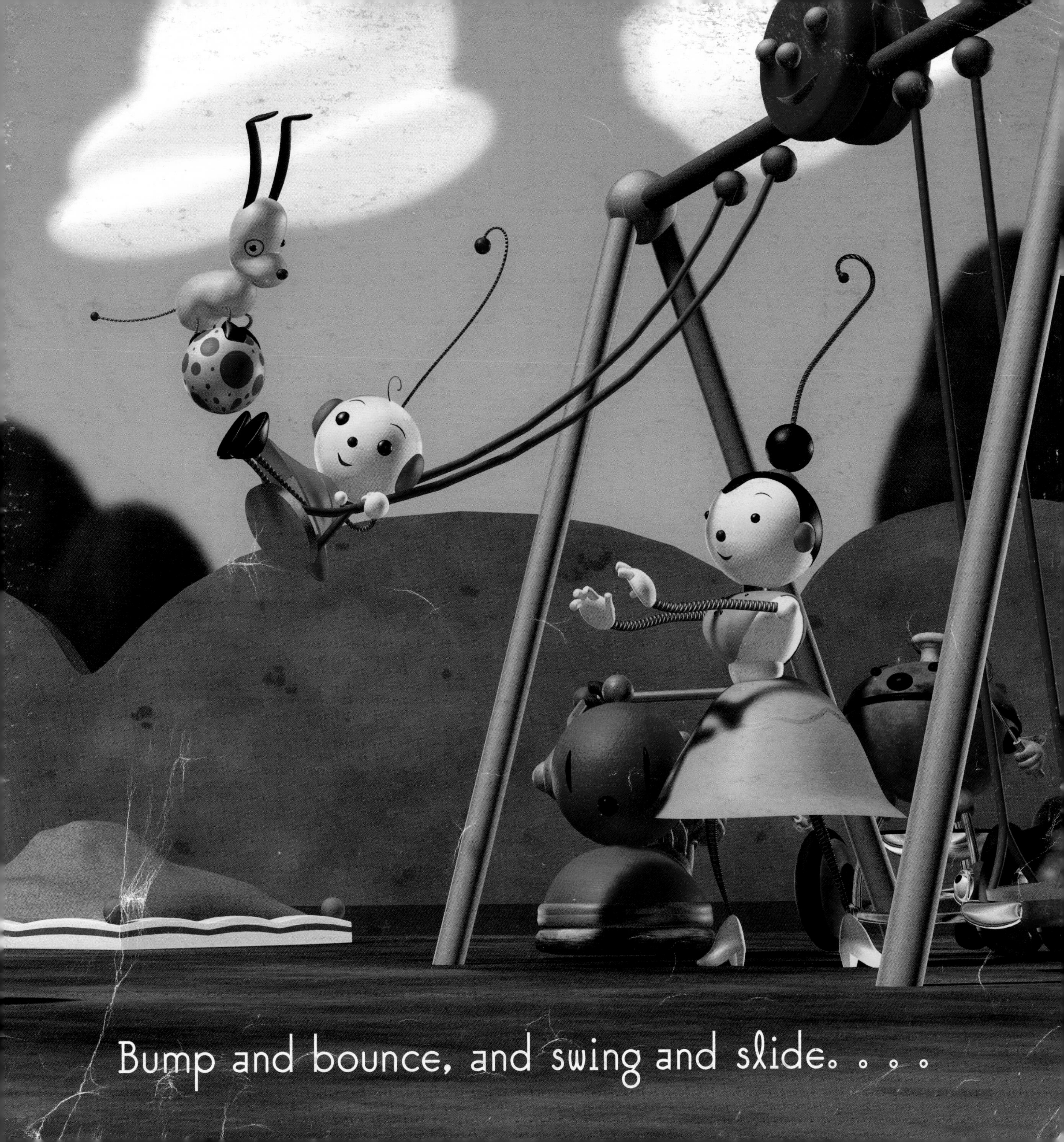

Bump and bounce, and swing and slide. . . .

Hidin',
seekin',
sneakin',
peekin'.

lookin',
    findin',
        step insidin'.

Jump up and up
and up so high—
You very nearly
Rolie fly!

"Not too high,"
said Dad atop
the tree house
where he'd gone
kerplop!

You're Rolie hot and Polie tired.
Your motor's zapped.
Your piston's fired.

Yes, okey dokey is the day
when all you Rolie did was play.
Hip,
   hip,
      hip,
         hip,
            hip . . .

HOORAY!

Daylight ended.

Evening came.

Time to play

the bedtime game.

But Olie was so wild and wired,
his batteries were not yet tired.
"I'm not sleepy!" Olie said,
"and I will **never** go to bed!"

He clanked and crashed,
turned rooms to rubble.
He stamped and stomped
then popped Zo's bubble . . .

. . . and got into a bunch of trouble.

So no good-nights,

no tuckin' in.

Just frowns where Rolie grins had been.

He rolled up in his Rolie bed.

He thought awhile

and scratched his head.

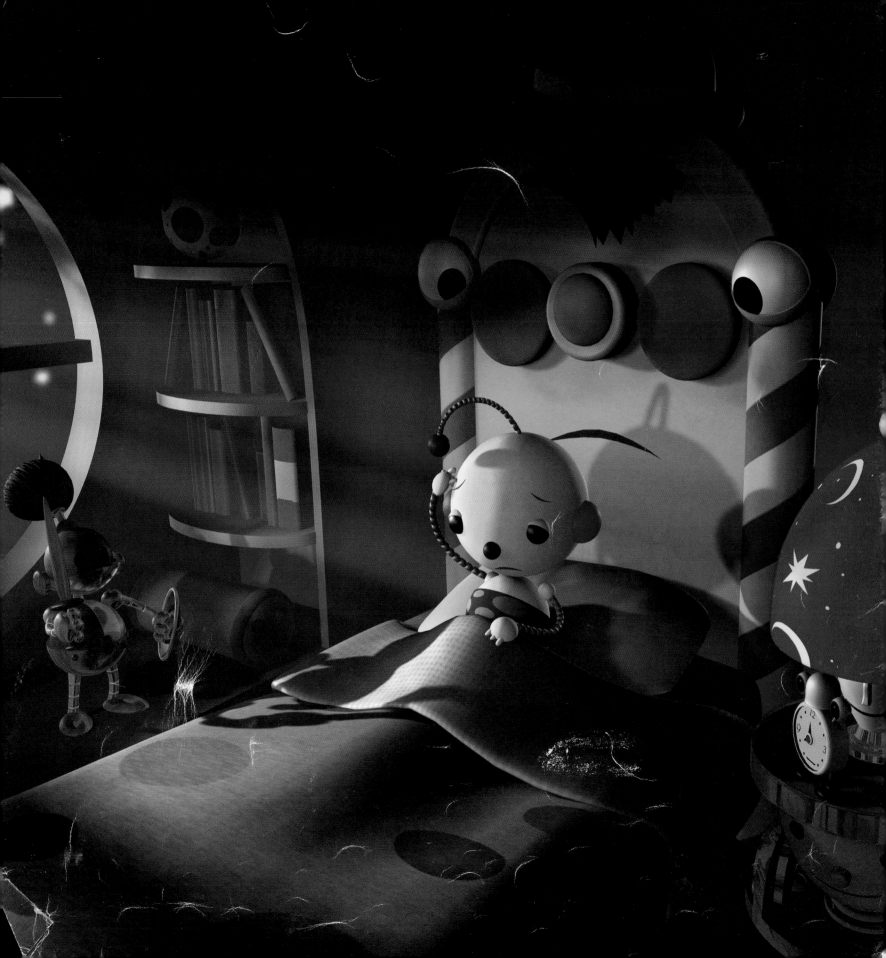

"Where's my
Rolie Momma?
Where's my Rolie Dad?
The world's so round
and lonely, and I'm
Rolie Polie sad."

There was Rolie Momma!

There was Rolie Pop!

There was Rolie Zowie!

There was even Rolie Spot!

"Sorry, Rolie Momma.

Sorry, Rolie Pop."

Then he stopped and looked at Zowie,

and he kissed her Rolie top.

Safe and snug and sleepy, tucked tightly into bed. . . . Sweet round and Rolie dreams swirled in every Rolie head.

Next morning, they rolled out of bed.

Brushed their teeth.

Recharged their heads.

The Rolie Polie Rumba Dance

was danced *again* in underpants!

Date Due